# Outdoors

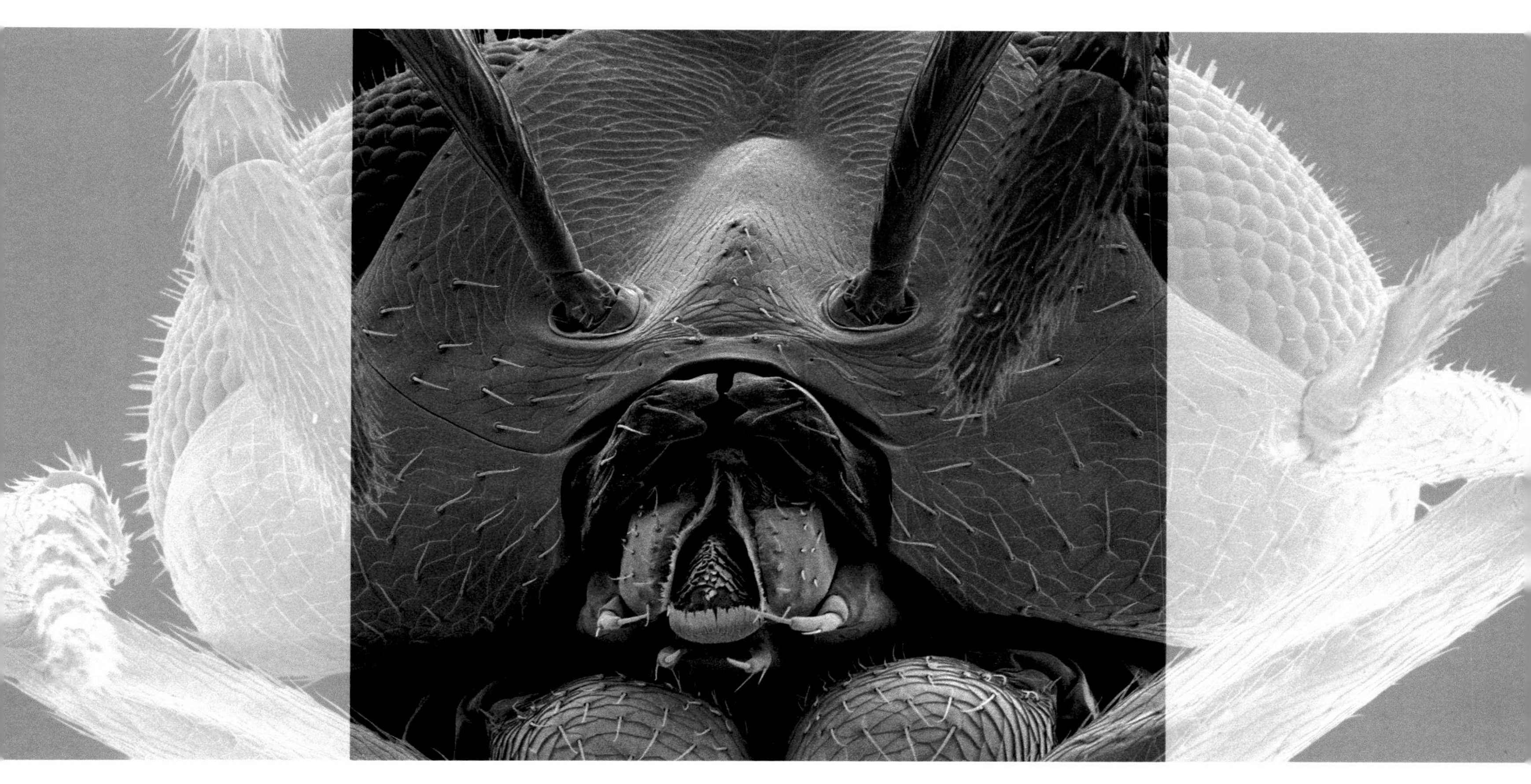

Sabrina Crewe

Franklin Watts
First published in Great Britain in 2016 by The Watts Publishing Group



Credits
Series editor: Paul Humphrey
Series designer: sprout.uk.com
Planning and production by Discovery Books Limited
Design and illustration: sprout.uk.com

Photo credits: Blickwinkel/Alamy Stock Photo: 18–19; Bigstock: 4, 5, 6, 9, 10, 13, 14, 16, 18, 19, 23, 25, 27, 28, 29; Biophoto Associates/Science Photo Library: 26–27; Jeremy Burgess/Science Photo Library: 28–29; Kenneth Eward/Biografx/Science Photo Library: 4–5; Roger Griffith: 12, 21; Steve Gschmeissner/Science Photo Library: title page, 10–11, 24–25; Gerd Guenther/Science Photo Library: 20–21; Power & Syred/Science Photo Library: 3, 6–7, 12–13, 14–15; Keith Wheeler/Science Photo Library: 8–9, 22–23; USDA: front cover, 16–17.



ISBN 978 1 4451 5111 3

Printed in China

MIX
Paper from responsible sources
FSC® C104740



Franklin Watts
An imprint of
Hachette Children's Group
Part of The Watts Publishing Group
Carmelite House
50 Victoria Embankment
London EC4Y 0DZ

An Hachette UK Company
www.hachette.co.uk

www.franklinwatts.co.uk

Note to the reader: many SEM images use false colours to make the subject more visible. Whenever possible the magnification of images has been added.

# Contents



Words in **bold** can be found in the glossary on page 30.

# The world of micro monsters

**You probably think a garden or park is a peaceful place. Flowers are growing, birds are chirping, bees are buzzing and water is trickling .... Think again. There's a world of monsters out there – micro monsters!**

Tiny living things that you can see only under a microscope are called **microorganisms**. Some of them are micro-animals: insects and other creatures too small to see without a microscope. Other microorganisms are **microbes**: micro-**fungi** and **bacteria** so tiny that you need super-strong microscopes to see them.

Scanning electron microscopes (SEMs) can magnify things many thousands of times. The world's most powerful microscope can magnify things up to thirty million times. Let's look at some of the micro monsters that SEMs can show us.

**Another world appears when you look into a microscope.**

## Needling nematodes

A good place to start is with nematodes. There are billions of these micro-animals in the soil of most gardens. The pin nematode (below) is named for the nasty pin-like weapon it uses to pierce the roots of plants to feed from them. If lots of them feed on one plant, they can damage it.

### Gross or what?

**In a handful of soil, there could be hundreds of nematodes, many metres of fungi and millions of microbes!**

## Monstrous data

| | |
|---|---|
| **Name** | **Pin nematode** |
| **Latin name** | ***Paratylenchus projectus*** |
| **Adult length** | **0.3–0.4 millimetres (mm)** |
| **Habitat** | **Moist soil near plant roots** |
| **Lifespan** | **Less than 30 days** |

**Many nematodes and other microorganisms have an important job to do in the garden. They help plants grow and keep soil healthy. They do this by breaking down plant matter, helping air and water move through soil and adding nutrients.**

# Water bears

**Tardigrades, or water bears, can survive in just about every extreme environment you can think of. They've been boiled, frozen, squashed and even sent into space.**

These indestructible micro monsters have been found everywhere from the highest mountains to the deepest oceans, and yet they are just as likely to be in your local park. Tardigrades love water, but if the water dries up, so do they. Tardigrades simply tuck in their head and legs, curl up and call it quits. The dry, wrinkly bundle they become is called a tun. They stay just like that until they get watered, and then they start to move again.

## Monstrous data

| | |
|---|---|
| **Name** | **Tardigrade** |
| **Latin name** | ***Tardigrada*** |
| **Adult length** | **0.3–1.5 mm** |
| **Habitat** | **Moss or lichen** |
| **Lifespan** | **Up to 10 years** |

**Tardigrades eat other micro-animals and moss. Otherwise they have no effect on the garden or on people.**

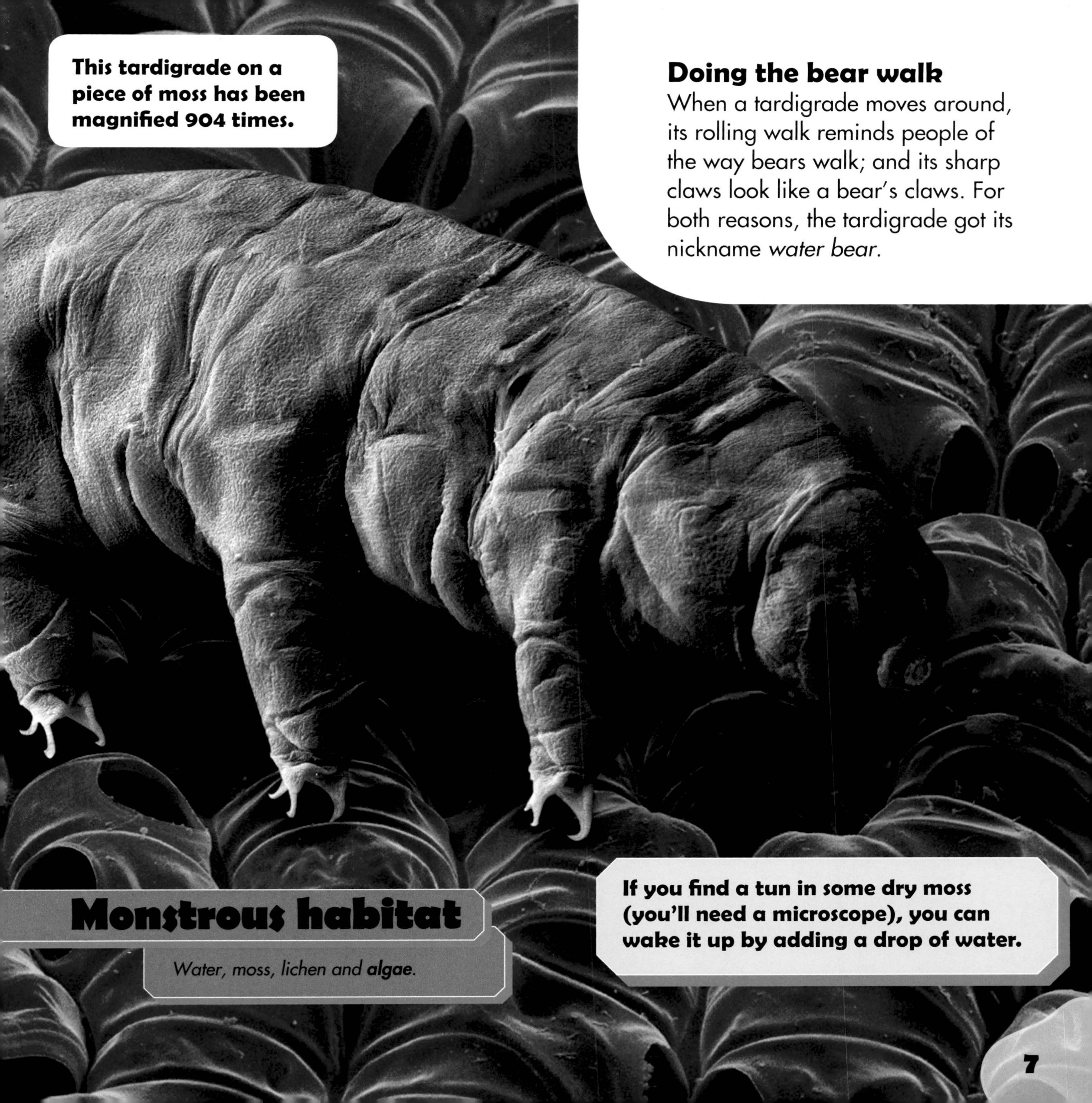

**This tardigrade on a piece of moss has been magnified 904 times.**

## Doing the bear walk

When a tardigrade moves around, its rolling walk reminds people of the way bears walk; and its sharp claws look like a bear's claws. For both reasons, the tardigrade got its nickname *water bear*.

## Monstrous habitat

*Water, moss, lichen and* ***algae****.*

**If you find a tun in some dry moss (you'll need a microscope), you can wake it up by adding a drop of water.**

# Hydra hunters

**If you were a water flea, you wouldn't want to run into a hydra when you were out for a swim. This water flea (on the right in a tangle of algae) is about to find out why.**

The horrible hydra has **tentacles** around its mouth, each one covered in stinging **cells**. The cells hold pointy poisonous darts at the end of a coiled thread. When the hydra finds its **prey**, it triggers the cells – sometimes hundreds of them – and out pop the poisoned darts. The poison **paralyses** the prey, the tentacles surround it and the hydra swallows it up!

Hydra

## Monstrous data

| | |
|---|---|
| **Name** | **Hydra** |
| **Latin name** | ***Hydra*** |
| **Adult length** | **2 mm** |
| **Habitat** | **Watery spots** |
| **Lifespan** | **In theory, forever!** |

## Gross or what?

**When it's time to reproduce, a hydra just grows a bud out of its side. The bud turns into a mini version of its parent. Spot the mini-monsters growing on this hydra!**

**The hydra comes from the same family as the jellyfish.**

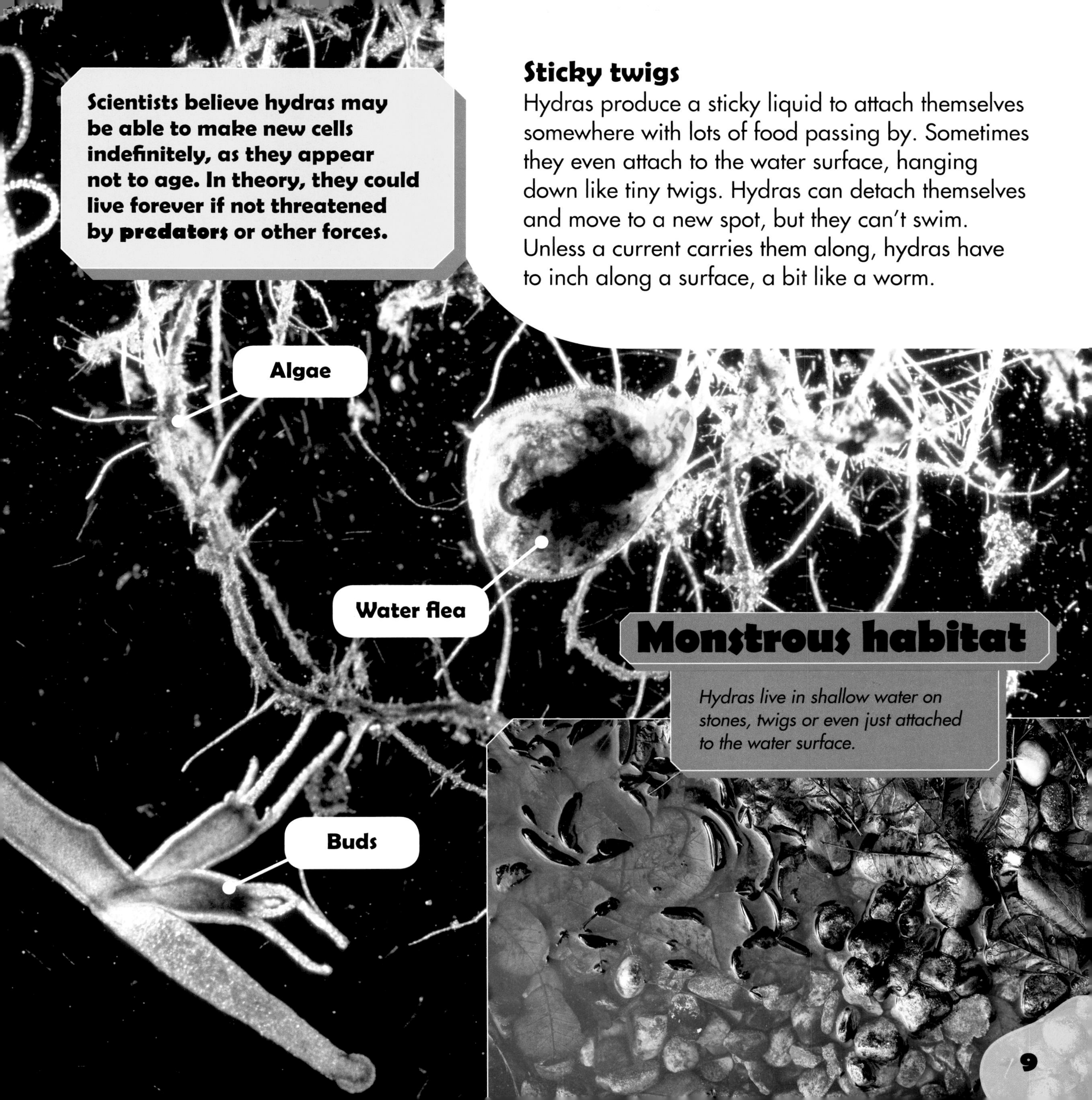


**Scientists believe hydras may be able to make new cells indefinitely, as they appear not to age. In theory, they could live forever if not threatened by predators or other forces.**

## Sticky twigs

Hydras produce a sticky liquid to attach themselves somewhere with lots of food passing by. Sometimes they even attach to the water surface, hanging down like tiny twigs. Hydras can detach themselves and move to a new spot, but they can't swim. Unless a current carries them along, hydras have to inch along a surface, a bit like a worm.

## Monstrous habitat

*Hydras live in shallow water on stones, twigs or even just attached to the water surface.*

# Insect invaders

**If there's one thing pests in the park fear more than bug spray, it's a pest parasite! Parasites live in or on other living things called hosts. Parasites that kill their hosts are called parasitoids. Parasitoid wasps live in small outdoor animals, from ants and beetles to spiders and moths.**

Many of these micro monsters use their eggs to invade their hosts. Female wasps lay their eggs inside an **aphid** or caterpillar or whatever creature they fancy most. The eggs hatch and become **larvae**. Then the larvae start to munch on the host from the inside out. Ouch!

## Monstrous habitat

*Parasitoid wasp larvae live in their host until they **pupate**, or become adults. Then many live around plants like this cabbage, where they can find their own hosts.*

## Monstrous data

| Name | Parasitoid wasp |
| --- | --- |
| Latin name | *Aphelinus abdominalis* |
| Adult length | Up to 1 mm |
| Habitat | On pests that live in or on plants |
| Lifespan | A few weeks |

**Parasitic wasps can kill pests that damage crops. The wasp in this photo is used to control aphids on potatoes and other plants.**

## Fighting back

Other insects don't take the invasion lying down. They may grow thick shells that stop the wasps from getting in. Some wriggle and wiggle to get the parasite off. Others might bite, poison, or even vomit on their parasites!

**Even parasites have parasites! These oh-so-tiny invaders are called hyperparasites.**

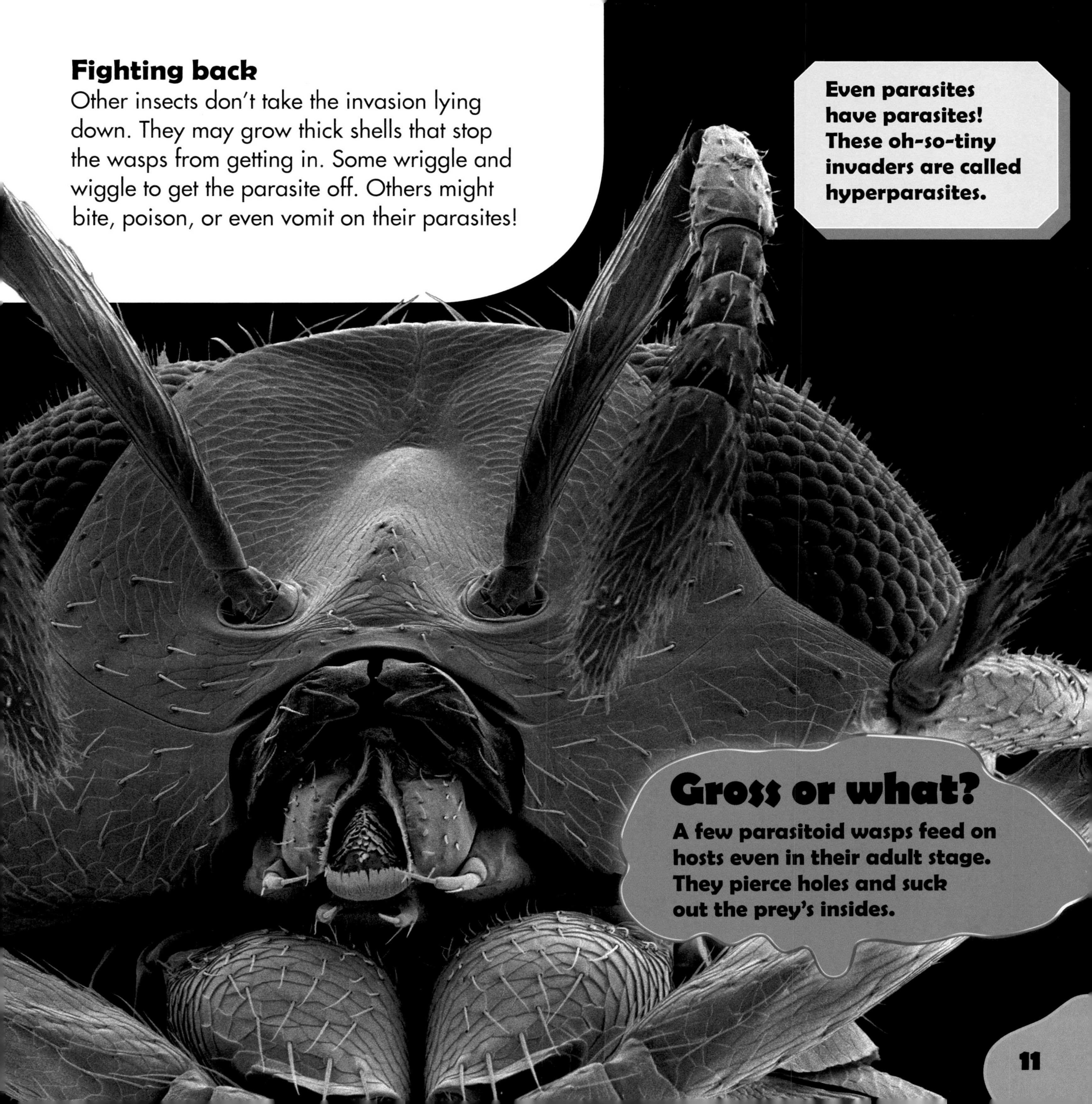

## Gross or what?

**A few parasitoid wasps feed on hosts even in their adult stage. They pierce holes and suck out the prey's insides.**

# Mighty mites

**Gall mites feed on plant cells, the tiny parts that plants are made up of. When these mighty micro monsters pierce a leaf on a tree, the leaf cells around the mite get bigger. The cells form bumps and lumps, fluffy looking balls or even spiny red fingers. These extra parts are called galls.**

Gall mites are **arachnids**, a group of creatures that includes spiders.

The gall mite lays its eggs inside the gall. The eggs hatch, and the young mites grow inside the gall. When the mites are all grown up, the gall dries up and splits open. Out come the mites, ready to start searching for their own juicy leaf. Many gall mites spend the winter in tree buds or bark.

## Gross or what?

**When one of these galls (below) splits open, hundreds of micro-mites will come out.**

## Monstrous habitat

*Gall mites live on trees and smaller plants. Young gall mites hatch and live inside galls.*

**Some gall mites drool chemicals into the leaves they feed on. This chemical makes the gall grow.**

**This SEM image of gall mites shows them magnified 2,362 times.**

# Monstrous data

| | |
|---|---|
| **Name** | **Gall mite** |
| **Latin name** | ***Eriophyes*** |
| **Adult length** | **0.15–0.5 mm** |
| **Habitat** | **Leaves and tree trunks** |
| **Lifespan** | **Up to one year** |

## Damage control

Galls can make leaves curl and flowers look funny. People use all kinds of stuff to get rid of them. But they don't do any real harm to the plant.

# Amazing amoebas

**Amoebas might look like tiny harmless blobs, but they have some nasty habits. The blue-green amoeba shown here is slowly advancing on the mauve amoeba. Before long, the mauve blob will be no more.**

Even though they have only one cell, amoebas have feet – false feet, that is. These jellied extensions help them ooze along. The feet flow in the general direction of where the amoeba wants to go, and then the rest of the amoeba catches up. Its false feet are about to reach the mauve amoeba and absorb it (take it in). The mauve amoeba will be eaten by the blue-green amoeba.

## Monstrous data

| Name | Amoeba |
|---|---|
| Latin name | ***Amoeba proteus*** |
| Adult length | 0.2–0.4 mm |
| Habitat | Watery places |
| Lifespan | Up to one year |

## Monstrous habitat

*Amoebas live everywhere in water and on the bottom of ponds, fountains and puddles.*

## Divide and double

Amoebas are one-celled **protozoa**. Their cell, like the cells in your body, has a **nucleus**. When it is ready to reproduce, the amoeba's nucleus simply divides into two and forms two separate and identical cells. Hey presto! Two amoebas for the price of one.

# Bee bloodsuckers

**The Varroa destructor, or honey bee mite, is a bloodsucking micro monster. Bee mites attach themselves to their buzzing hosts and feed on hemolymph, or bee blood. This is bad enough, but just for good measure the Varroa also carries some vile viruses. One virus paralyses the bee. Another stops its wings from growing properly.**

The female mite lays her eggs in the cell of the hive where the bee is growing. The eggs hatch and the young mites settle on the bee, feeding, growing and **mating**. When the bee leaves its cell, the mites leave right along with it. Out in the world, they often hop onto another passing bee, like the one below.

## Monstrous data

| | |
|---|---|
| Name | Varroa mite or honey bee mite |
| Latin name | *Varroa destructor* |
| Adult length | 1–1.5 mm |
| Habitat | In beehives and on bees |
| Lifespan | 2–8 months |

**Male mites die after mating in the bee's cell, so only females leave the cell with the bee.**

## Monstrous habitat

*Varroa mites live on bees all over the world, except in Australia (so far).*

**Pesticides used in farming also harm bees. Some scientists say farmers and gardeners should instead protect crops with pest-eating bugs, such as ladybirds.**

## Mighty mystery

A few years ago, bees all over the world started dying out. If bees die, plants don't get **pollinated**. That's a serious threat to plants we grow for food, such as wheat. Scientists aren't sure of all the reasons. But they do know some of the bees were dying because of the mite and the viruses it carries. It's not called *destructor* for nothing!

## Gross or what?

**Because bee mites are flat, they can hide in the folds of a bee's body. Bet you're glad you're not a bee!**

# One-eyed monsters

**Take a look in a pond, or even a puddle of water in the park. Imagine a one-eyed shrimp swimming there, so small you can't see it. What you're imagining is a cyclops. This mini-crustacean might actually be in the puddle at your feet!**

The cyclops is a copepod, a tiny crustacean. (Big crustaceans are shellfish, such as lobsters.) They have five pairs of legs, which are quite hard to see, a large pair of antennae (feelers) and one big eye smack in the middle of their heads.

**When a male cyclops wants to mate, he grasps a female with his antennae.**

## Monstrous data

| | |
|---|---|
| **Name** | **Cyclops** |
| **Latin name** | ***Cyclopoida*** |
| **Adult length** | **1–2 mm** |
| **Habitat** | **Any body of water** |
| **Lifespan** | **3 months** |

## Monstrous habitat

*Cyclops live in all types of water – even just a few drops are enough to be home to cyclops.*

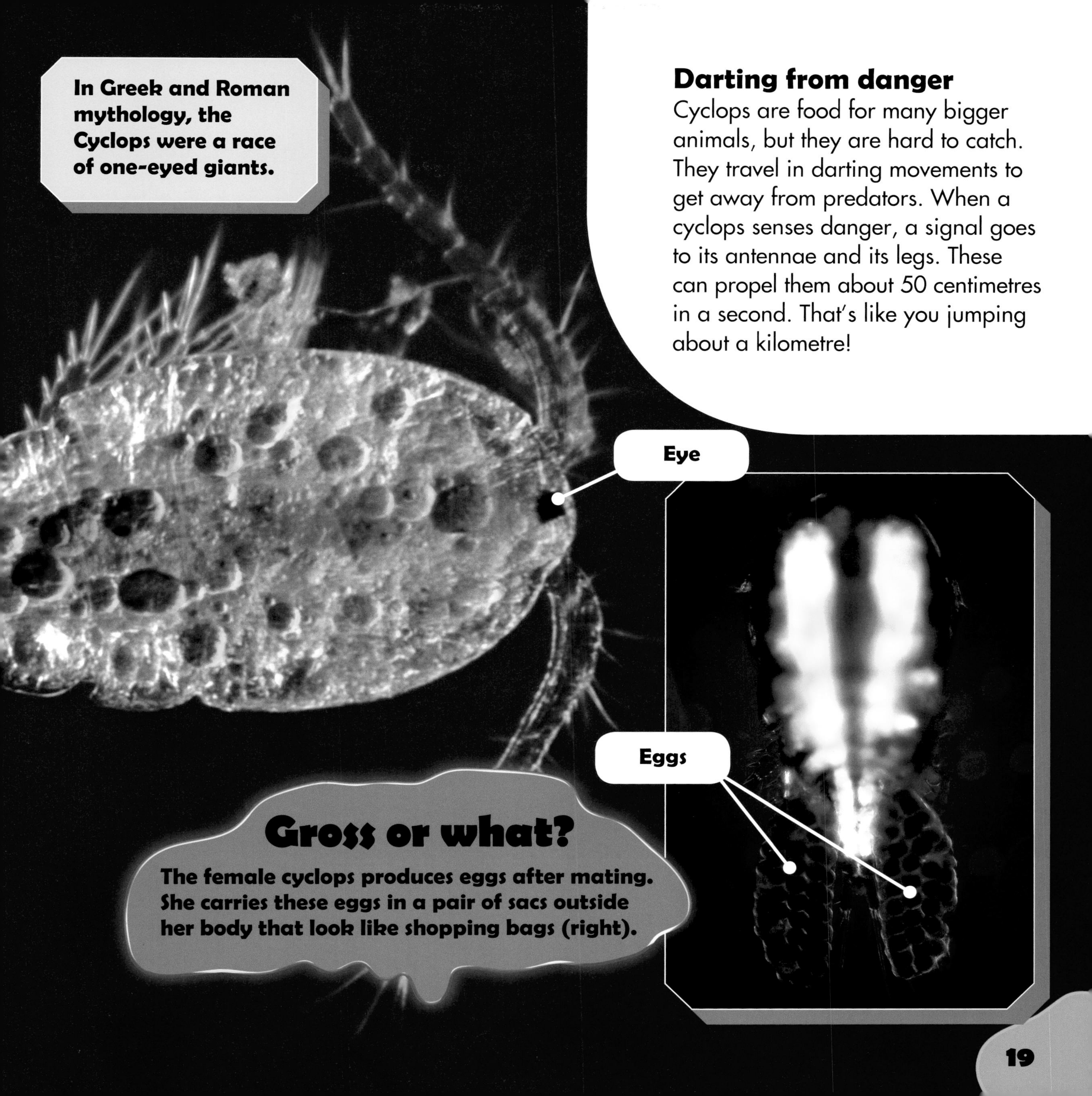


## Darting from danger

Cyclops are food for many bigger animals, but they are hard to catch. They travel in darting movements to get away from predators. When a cyclops senses danger, a signal goes to its antennae and its legs. These can propel them about 50 centimetres in a second. That's like you jumping about a kilometre!

## Gross or what?

**The female cyclops produces eggs after mating. She carries these eggs in a pair of sacs outside her body that look like shopping bags (right).**

# Powder power

**What's this micro monster doing? Believe it or not, this is a fungus spitting out its spores! Spores are what fungi produce instead of seeds. When they are ripe, spores burst out of the fungus. They fly through the air to land on surfaces where they can spread.**

Every now and then, you probably notice a dusting of white powder on leaves in the park. This is a fungus called powdery mildew, shown here. Fungi are living **organisms**, like plants, except they can't make their own food. So fungi weave wicked webs of **hyphae**, tiny threads that feed off plants and sprout fruiting bodies (pods full of spores).

**Powdery mildew can harm plants, but most fungi are good for the garden. They break down dead matter as they feed on it, turning it into nutrients for the soil.**

## Monstrous data

| | |
|---|---|
| **Name** | **Powdery mildew** |
| **Latin name** | ***Microsphaera alphitoides*** |
| **Adult length** | **0.15 mm** |
| **Habitat** | **Horse chestnut and oak trees** |
| **Lifespan** | **1 day–1 month** |

## Gross or what?

**In tropical gardens, there are fungi that invade the bodies of ants and other insects. They grow on their host in the form of toadstools or hairs. Bit by bit, the fungi replace their victim's cells with their own, until they kill it.**

# Monstrous habitat

*Fungi live on living and dead things, such as the leaves, flowers and roots of trees and smaller plants, including crops.*

**This powdery mildew has been magnified about 700 times.**

**So far, more than 45,000 kinds of fungi have been identified in soil.**

## Monster mushrooms

Powdery mildew is a micro-fungus, but fungi come in other forms. They can be anything from the mould on an old cheese sandwich to an edible mushroom to a giant puffball. In fact, the Latin word *fungus* means mushroom.

# Wheely wonders

**Under the water lilies in a pond lurks a strange and sticky micro monster. You can always spot a rotifer, or wheel animal, by the whirling wheels on the top of its head. Well, you could if it wasn't microscopic, of course!**

This floscularia is a type of rotifer. These spinning tops aren't just for decoration. Rotifers catch their prey by creating waves that make tiny bits of food drift into their gaping mouths. The wheel is made up of a crown of tiny hairs called cilia.

## Monstrous data

| | |
|---|---|
| **Name** | **Wheel animal or wheel bearer** |
| **Latin name** | ***Floscularia ringens*** |
| **Adult length** | **1 mm** |
| **Habitat** | **Still water** |
| **Lifespan** | **1–6 weeks** |

## Gross or what?

**The floscularia has a set of jaws somewhere between its mouth and its belly, with several rows of sharp fangs.**

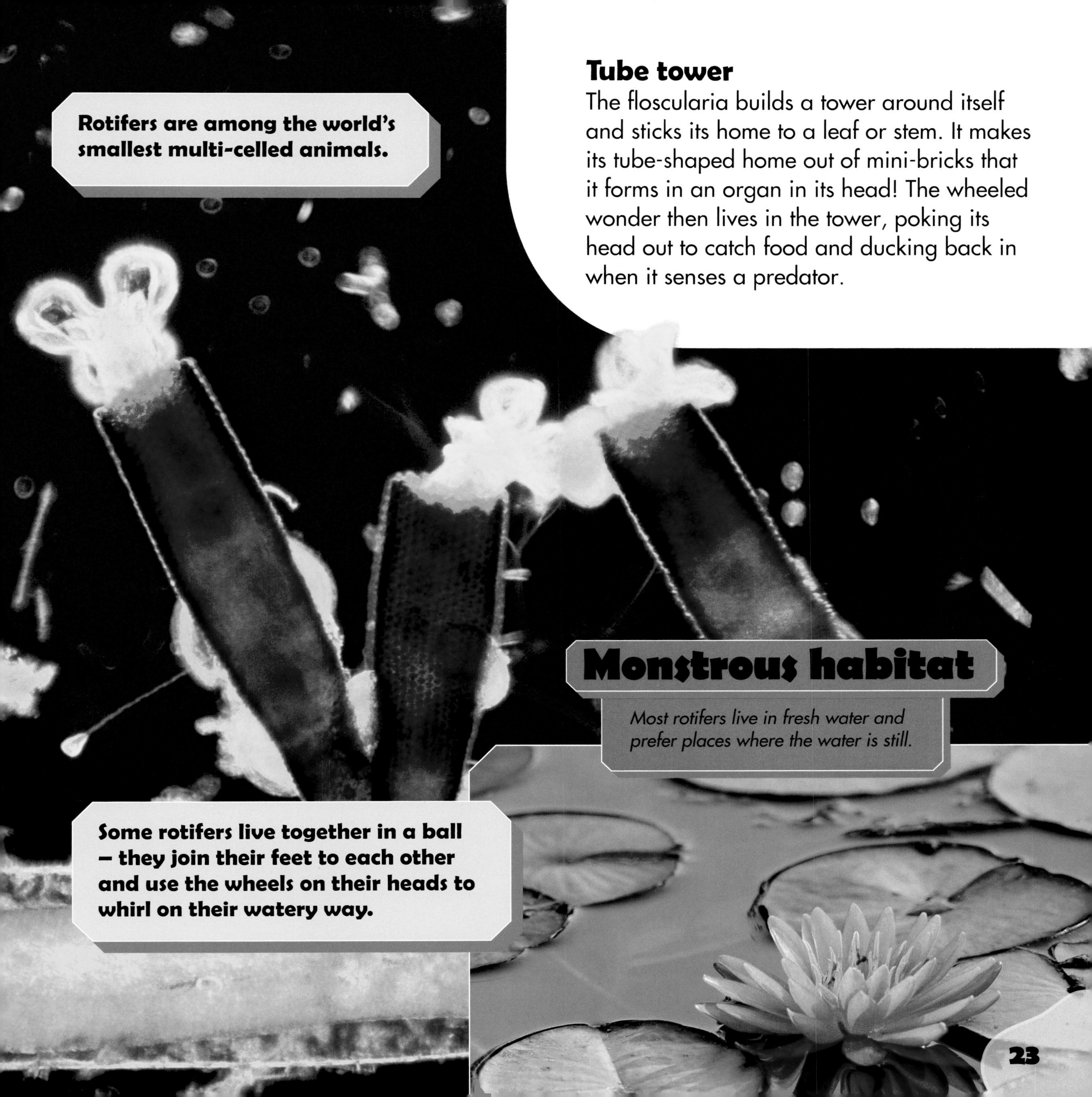

Rotifers are among the world's smallest multi-celled animals.

## Tube tower

The floscularia builds a tower around itself and sticks its home to a leaf or stem. It makes its tube-shaped home out of mini-bricks that it forms in an organ in its head! The wheeled wonder then lives in the tower, poking its head out to catch food and ducking back in when it senses a predator.

## Monstrous habitat

*Most rotifers live in fresh water and prefer places where the water is still.*

Some rotifers live together in a ball – they join their feet to each other and use the wheels on their heads to whirl on their watery way.

# Prickly or sticky?

**This spiky trichome looks pretty scary to microscopic munchers. It's supposed to! Leaves on many plants grow trichomes, parts of the plant that ward off mini-pests and bigger beasts, including you.**

Trichomes are often just one cell, but they come in many shapes. You probably couldn't see this tiny trichome, but you've seen little hairs sticking out of some leaves. Larger trichomes are visible to humans. Think of a stinging nettle. It's those tiny hairs you see that sting like crazy when you brush against the leaves. Trichomes also protect the plant from heat and cold or make the leaves unpleasant to eat.

**Some bees use trichomes to line their nest. They scrape the hairs off a leaf, bundle them up and carry them home.**

**Some super-stiff trichomes can stick to your clothes like burrs, bringing tiny plant parts with them. In this way, plant seeds hitch a ride to a new spot.**

## Monstrous data

| | |
|---|---|
| **Name** | **Trichome of a flannel bush leaf** |
| **Latin name** | ***Fremontodendron trichome*** |
| **Adult length** | **0.4 mm** |
| **Habitat** | **Leaf surface** |
| **Lifespan** | **One leaf season** |

## Gross or what?

**The sundew plant uses its sticky trichomes to capture microscopic bugs. Once a bug is stuck, the hungry sundew rolls up its prey in a leaf and gobbles it up.**

## Monstrous habitat

*Trichomes grow on leaves and other plant parts all over the world, as well as on some lichens and algae.*

### Fuzzy flannel

This sharp-looking trichome may ward off caterpillars, but it wouldn't feel spiky to you. The leaves feel fuzzy, like flannel fabric. That's why the plant (shown above) is called flannel bush. But don't rub flannel bush leaves. They can irritate your skin and your eyes.

**This trichome is magnified 420 times.**

# Hairy horrors

**Can you see what's happening here? A dastardly didinium is attacking and then swallowing another micro monster, a paramecium bigger than itself! Going, going, gone.**

The didinium is one of a group of organisms called ciliates. **Ciliates** are protozoa, a type of **protist**, which means they have only one cell.

**If the didinium can't get any food for a while, it covers itself in a shell and goes dormant until it senses some new prey.**

1. Didinium (top) catches its prey (bottom).

## Monstrous data

| | |
|---|---|
| Name | Didinium |
| Latin name | *Didinium nasutum* |
| Adult length | 50–150 micrometres |
| Habitat | Anywhere there is water |

## Gross or what?

**Didinium mostly eat other ciliates, such as the paramecium being devoured in these pictures. The didinium will digest its food in a few hours and be ready to**

## Not so silly cilia

Cilia are pretty useful if you're a ciliate. They help with just about everything. Some cilia are used like little oars for swimming and for stopping. Other cilia sense or catch prey, and some kinds wave prey in the general direction of a hungry ciliate's mouth. Still others help their owners attach to or crawl along a surface.

## Monstrous habitat

*Ciliates live in water in ponds, puddles and drops of water in garden soil.*

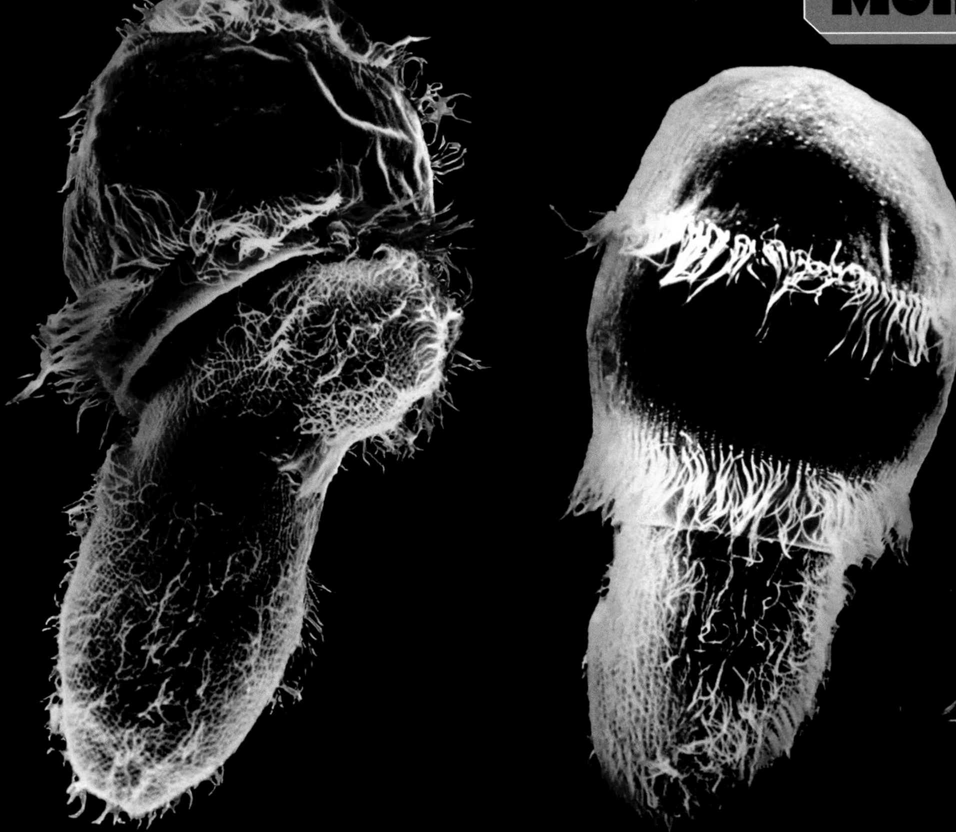

**2. Didinium swallows prey.**

**3. Prey is half-devoured.**

**4. Goodbye paramecium!**

***Proto* means first, or original, and *zoa* means animals, so protozoa means 'first animals'. Even though protozoa are not really animals, they behave like them by hunting prey.**

# Busy bacteria

This SEM image of a root nodule is magnified 394 times.

**As you've realised by now, a peaceful garden or park is actually a heaving universe of invisible creepy crawlies, miniature monsters and pin-sized parasites. While these creatures are busy destroying plants and each other, the tiniest of microbes are doing most of the gardening.**

This funny-looking pink lump (right) is actually a tiny nodule (growth) on the root of a pea plant. Inside it, millions of bacteria are working away. Bacteria are made of a single cell and usually live on other things in clumps or groups, multiplying like mad. In fact, rhizobium bacteria made this nodule by multiplying and swelling as they fed off the plant.

## Monstrous data

| | |
|---|---|
| Name | Nitrogen-fixing bacteria |
| Latin name | *Rhizobium leguminosarum* |
| Adult length | Less than 2 micrometres |
| Habitat | Roots of plants |
| Lifespan | Constantly dividing and multiplying |

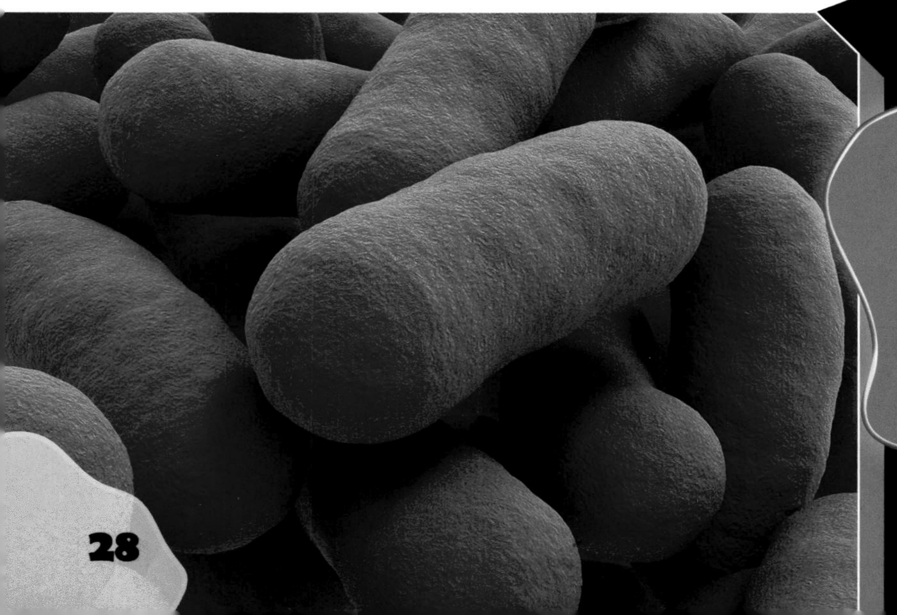

## Gross or what?

You've probably been infected by bacteria at some time, with an ear or throat infection. Rhizobium bacteria are a kind of infection, too. Bullet-shaped bacteria like these on the left (magnified thousands of times) infect the plant by getting in through its root hairs.

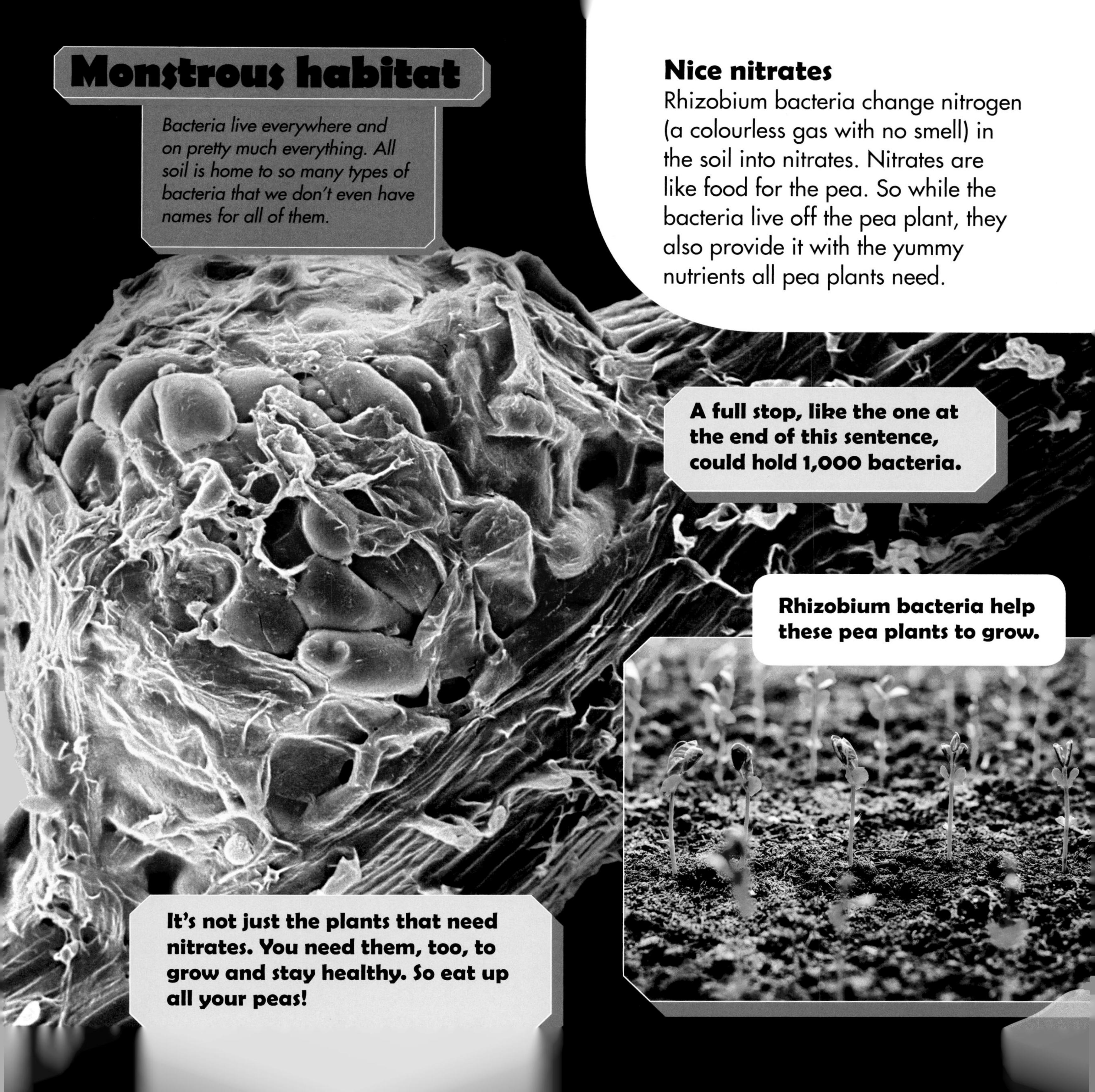

## Monstrous habitat

*Bacteria live everywhere and on pretty much everything. All soil is home to so many types of bacteria that we don't even have names for all of them.*

### Nice nitrates

Rhizobium bacteria change nitrogen (a colourless gas with no smell) in the soil into nitrates. Nitrates are like food for the pea. So while the bacteria live off the pea plant, they also provide it with the yummy nutrients all pea plants need.

**A full stop, like the one at the end of this sentence, could hold 1,000 bacteria.**

**Rhizobium bacteria help these pea plants to grow.**

**It's not just the plants that need nitrates. You need them, too, to grow and stay healthy. So eat up all your peas!**

# Glossary

**algae** organisms, including seaweeds, that are similar to plants

**amoeba** one-celled protozoa, or animal-like protist

**aphid** a tiny insect that lives on plants

**arachnid** group of small animals, including spiders and mites, with eight legs and two parts to their bodies

**bacteria** one-celled organisms that are the most numerous living things in the world

**cell** the tiny unit that living things are made of, or the small unit of a beehive inside which bee larvae grow

**ciliate** a group of protozoa that have cilia, tiny hairs used for swimming and catching prey

**crops** plants grown for food

**crustacean** group of animals, most of which live in water and have an exterior skeleton that forms a hard shell

**dormant** the inactive state of living things when they are not moving, feeding or reproducing

**fungus** (pl: fungi) an organism that lives on and feeds off live or dead organic matter and reproduces with spores. Mushrooms and mildew are both fungi

**gall** an overgrown cell clump formed on plants by mites or other parasites

**habitat** the place or type of place where an organism usually lives

**host** an organism that is home to a parasite or a cell that is home to a virus

**hyphae** threads some fungi use to spread on their host

**larva** stage of an insect between egg and adult

**lichen** an organism that looks like a plant, but is in fact made up of combined algae and fungi

**mate** join together to reproduce

**microbe** any microscopic living thing that is not an animal

**micrometre** the measurement of length that is one-thousandth of a millimetre and sometimes called a micron

**microorganism** a living thing too small to see without a microscope

**microscopic** too small to see without a microscope

**nucleus** the headquarters of a cell

**nutrient** substance that organisms need to survive and grow

**organism** any living or formerly living thing

**paralyse** make something unable to move

**parasite** a living thing that lives on or in another living thing and uses its host as food

**pesticide** a chemical that kills pests

**pollinate** to carry pollen from one plant to another

**predator** an animal or microbe that hunts prey for food

**prey** an animal or microbe hunted and caught for food

**protist** an organism, usually with only one cell, that is neither a plant nor animal but is often similar to one or the other

**protozoa** protists (single-celled organisms) that are similar to animals

**pupate** become a pupa, a stage of an insect's life during which it changes into an adult

**reproduce** to make new living things

**rotifer** a micro-animal with cilia on its head

**spore** a plant or fungus cell that can develop into a new plant or fungus

**tentacle** long, thin body part that sticks out from an animal's head and is used to sense or grasp things

**virus** a microbe that multiplies by infecting the cells of organisms

# Further information

### Books

**Complete Book of the Microscope**
*by Kirsteen Rogers* (Usborne, 2012)

**Horrible Science: Microscopic Monsters**
*by Nick Arnold* (Scholastic, 2014)

**In the Backyard (Under the Microscope)**
*by Sabrina Crewe* (Chelsea Clubhouse, 2010)

### Websites

**http://tardigrades.bio.unc.edu**
*You can find movies, photos and everything about tardigrades here.*

**http://www.uglybug.org/06dex.shtml**
*Quite a collection of bug close-ups in this Ugly Bug Contest!*

**http://commtechlab.msu.edu/sites/dlc-me/zoo/index.html**
*Take a trip through the Microbe Zoo!*

**http://njarb.com/2012/11/100-amazing-electron-microscope-images/#plan**
*Amazing plant and animal pictures from the Science Photo Library collection.*

**https://microcosmos.foldscope.com**
*See images through a special microscope called a foldscope. The foldscope is made from folded paper, and each one costs just a few pence.*

*Every effort has been made by the publisher to ensure that these websites contain no inappropriate or offensive material. However, because of the nature of the Internet, it is impossible to guarantee that the content of these sites will not be altered. We strongly advise that Internet access is supervised by a responsible adult.*

### Measuring the microscopic world

It's hard to imagine how small micrometres and nanometres really are. This picture helps you to see how they compare to a millimetre. Millimetres are pretty tiny themselves, but they are GIANT compared to nanometres. In every millimetre, there are one million nanometres!

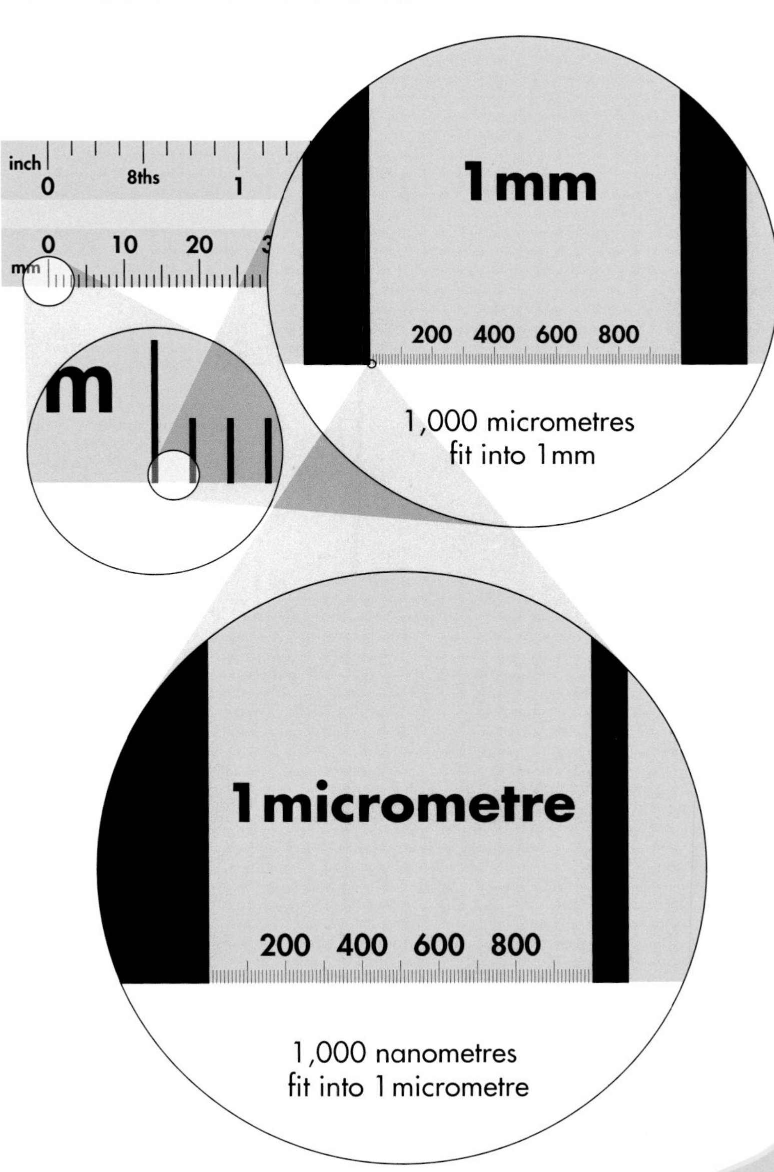

# Index

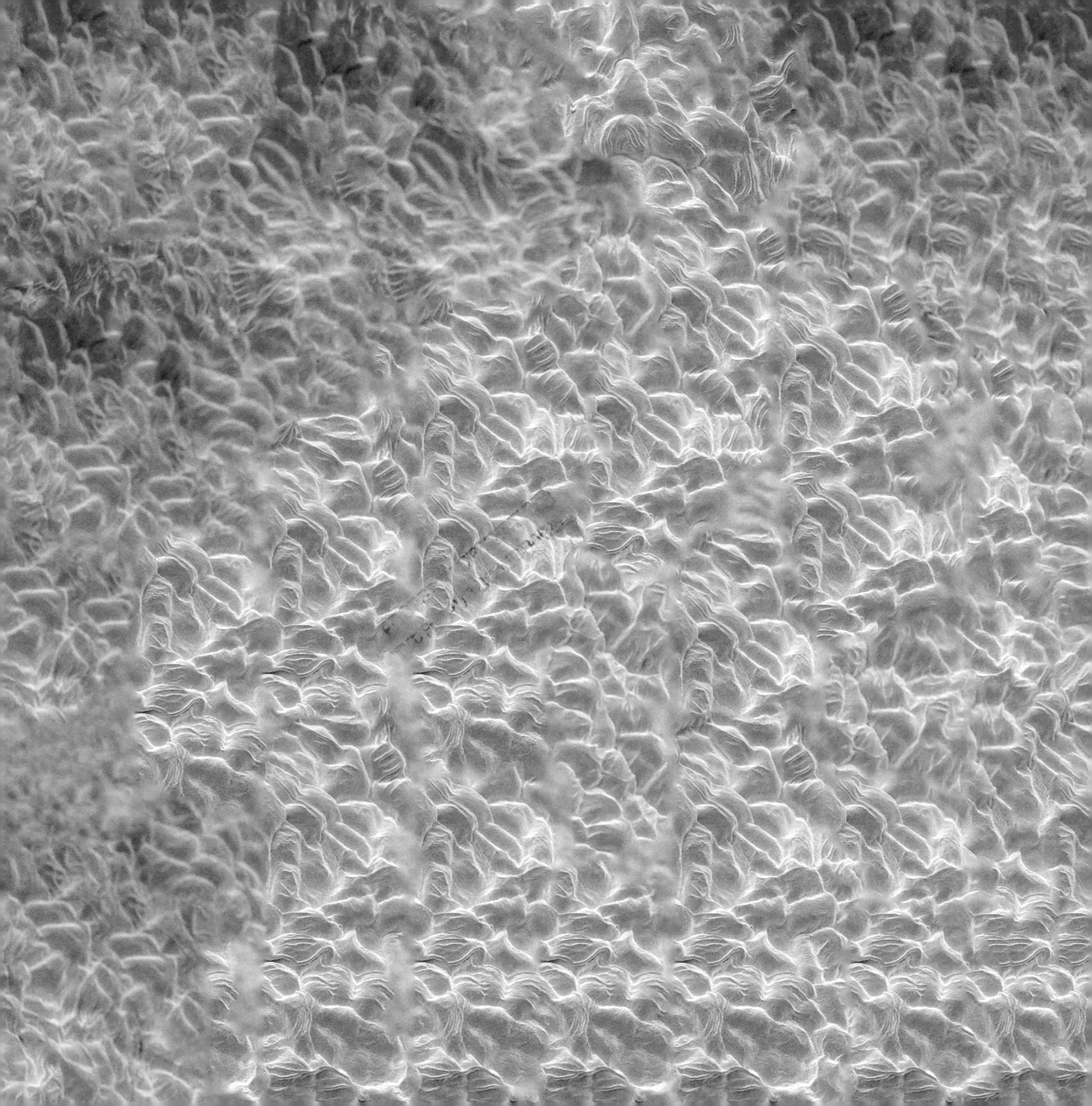